# HORSE DIARIES

*Special Edition*

## · Jingle Bells ·

HORSE DIARIES

# HORSE DIARIES

*Special Edition*

## Jingle Bells

CATHERINE HAPKA

illustrated by RUTH SANDERSON

RANDOM HOUSE 🏠 NEW YORK

Text copyright © 2014 by Catherine Hapka
Cover art and interior illustrations copyright © 2014 by Ruth Sanderson
Photograph credits: © Bob Langrish (p. 165); © Chad Ehlers/Alamy (p. 169);
Library of Congress (p. 170)

Visit us on the Web! randomhouse.com/kids

Educators and librarians, for a variety of teaching tools, visit us at
RHTeachersLibrarians.com

*Library of Congress Cataloging-in-Publication Data*
Hapka, Cathy.
Jingle Bells / Catherine Hapka ; illustrated by Ruth Sanderson.
pages cm. — (Horse diaries)
Summary: In 1915 Wisconsin, a farm horse named Jingle Bells worries
that his family will replace him when the older son brings home
a brand new Model T Ford car. Includes facts about Clydesdale horses.
ISBN 978-0-385-38484-1 (pbk.) — ISBN 978-0-385-38485-8 (lib. bdg.) —
ISBN 978-0-385-38486-5 (ebook)
1. Clydesdale horse—Juvenile fiction. [1. Clydesdale horse—Fiction.
2. Horses—Fiction. 3. Farm life—Fiction.] I. Sanderson, Ruth, illustrator. II. Title.
PZ10.3.H2258 Ji 2014 [Fic]—dc23 2013033336

Printed in the United States of America
10 9 8 7 6 5 4 3 2 1
First Edition

For Gerri and Annabelle and
Suzie and Claire and all the other good,
hardworking draft horses I've known

—C.H.


With thanks to
Blue Star Equiculture,
a draft horse rescue facility
in Palmer, Massachusetts

—R.S.

# CONTENTS

"Oh! if people knew what a comfort to horses a light hand is . . ."

—from *Black Beauty,* by Anna Sewell

# HORSE DIARIES

*Special Edition*

· Jingle Bells ·

# Wisconsin, Summer, 1915

My muscles strained against the harness as the hay wagon reached the spot where the ground sloped up on the way to the barn. The heavy summer air was filled with sounds—the wagon's wooden wheels creaked, a fly buzzed near my eyes, cows lowed in the distance, the mare harnessed beside me breathed in and out. But I ignored all except my master's voice as he spoke behind me.

"Good man, Jingle!" he called out. "There's a good horse."

My master, known as Lars, was a lean, weather-beaten man with kind eyes and gentle hands. I flicked an ear back at the sound of my name, then leaned forward, throwing my massive weight against the load. Sweat dripped down my sides as my hooves dug into the hard-packed dirt road. It was a hot day, close and still. On the horizon beyond the cow pasture, dark rain clouds were gathering.

Beside me, my harness partner sucked back. She was a young mare known as Millie—Silly Millie, the humans sometimes called her. *The load is too heavy,* she complained. *I can't pull any harder.*

*Yes, you can,* I replied. *We can always pull harder.*

Millie merely snorted in return. But I continued to put one feathered hoof in front of the other, and after a moment she leaned forward against her collar again, taking on her share of the load. The wagon rolled steadily up the hill.

We had been working hard all day, trying to bring in the last of the hay crop before the rain came. Lars and his second-eldest son, Jonas, had loaded the sweet-smelling greenish-gold bales into the wooden wagon. Millie and I had done our part, standing and waiting patiently between stops.

It was easy for me to be patient, but it was harder for Millie. She was only half draft, and her light horse side sometimes made her flighty. Then again, perhaps she was merely young. Even I had sometimes been silly in my youth. And I was all draft, a purebred Clydesdale—stout of limb, strong of heart, steady of temperament.

"Come up, Millie!" Jonas called, striding beside us. "Steady on, Jingle!" He was nearly as tall as his father, with the same pale hair and strong shoulders.

Finally we reached the top of the hill. From there, it was easy pulling to the large wooden barn. The farm dogs raced to greet us, barking and wagging their tails. The family's half-grown black-and-white kitten tumbled along behind the dogs. Millie snorted as a dog dashed beneath her feet, but I ignored its antics. Dogs were odd creatures, preferring to run when they could walk, and bark when they could be silent. But I was used to them and found little they did surprising anymore.

Two more of our master's children were rushing toward us, slower than the dogs but just as lively. One was Anders, the third son. But my gaze was trained on the other child, a bright-eyed girl called Kari. While I was fond of Lars and the rest of his family, his youngest daughter was special to me, and I to her. Sometimes Kari said that was because she'd given me my name: Jingle Bells. At other times, she claimed it was because we were the same age, eleven years.

I didn't know about any of that. But I knew that I especially liked the sight and sound and smell of Kari over all the others. I loved to feel her soft, gentle hands rubbing my nose or picking the knots out of my thick black mane.

"Careful, Mittens!" Anders scooped up the kitten as it batted at the feathers on my foreleg. "You'll get stepped on."

"Jingle would never," Kari informed him. "He's careful."

Lars hopped down from the wagon. "Leave that cat alone, and let's get to work," he said, casting an anxious glance at the sky. "Who knows how much longer the rain will hold off, and there's still the evening milking to do."

"Yes, Papa." Anders set the kitten down and hurried toward the wagon.

Kari followed. She was the only one of the family's three daughters who spent much time in the barn and fields, where she did her best to work just as hard as the boys. She was too small to lift a full bale of hay herself, but she could help

Anders push them off the wagon so that Lars and Jonas could stack them.

As the humans worked, Millie shifted her weight constantly from one foreleg to the other. *When will they finish?* she complained. *I'm hungry!*

*They'll finish when the work is done,* I replied. I cocked one hind foot and waited, ignoring the mare's fidgeting.

Finally the hay was where it was supposed to be. Lars and Jonas drove the wagon out of the way and unhitched us. Kari reached up toward my face as her father led me out of the traces, and I lowered my head and waited for her to grab the noseband of my bridle. She led me first to the water trough outside the barn, where I took a long drink. Anders brought Millie over, too, and we stood there together sucking in the cool water.

A vibrant blue dragonfly buzzed past and I lifted my head to watch it, water dripping from my muzzle. Then the colorful insect was gone, and I drank again.

"I'll give Jingle a good grooming, all right?" Kari said to her father.

"And I'll groom Millie," Anders offered.

"Thank you. The horses certainly earned their keep today." Lars removed his hat and swiped the sweat from his forehead with his arm. "Come, Jonas. Let's sweep out the wagon."

Kari tugged on my noseband again. I stepped away from the trough, following her into the barn and across to my stall. My steps were slow and deliberate, and I was careful to hold my head low, well below my withers. That was partly to avoid pulling Kari off the floor as she gripped my noseband—she weighed little more than that kitten, or so it seemed to me—and partly so I wouldn't step on her heels, or on the hens pecking for stray bits of grain on the floor, or on the kitten or the dogs, who as usual seemed to be everywhere at once as they accompanied us inside.

My stall felt shaded and cool compared to the heat outdoors. It was good to stand still and let the day's work seep out of my tired muscles. I lowered my head again so Kari could pull the collar off my neck, though she had to stand on a milking stool to peel the rest of the harness from my back and hindquarters. She staggered under the weight of the huge mound of leather and brass as she carried it out of the stall.

"Be right back, Jingle," she called over her shoulder.

She returned shortly with a grooming kit and climbed onto the milking stool again so she could reach my broad back with her stiff-bristled brush. She scrubbed the itchy sweat marks left by the collar and straps. It felt so good! My eyes drooped half-shut, and my lower lip flopped with pleasure.

"Poor Jingle—you're extra sweaty today! I wonder if this heat will ever end," Kari said. "It's terrible!"

Anders peeped through the plank wall separating my stall from Millie's. "Mama says the rain will help," he said. "But I'd rather have snow!"

Kari giggled. "Snow in summer? That will never happen!"

"Not here, maybe." Anders grinned, his blue eyes dancing. "But maybe in Norway it could happen. Mormor and Morfar's stories make it sound like it snowed there all year long when they were our age! Anyway, I'm only joking. Summer is better than winter any day."

"No way," Kari said. "I like winter better."

"You're crazy," Anders retorted. "Summer is the best! We go berry picking, catch fireflies, cool off in the swimming hole. . . ."

"And Papa never gets to sit down because he's so busy with the plowing and the haying and the calving and all the rest," Kari shot back. "The poor horses work just as hard, and we all spend our days sweating and miserably hot."

Anders snorted, sounding so much like a horse that I looked over in surprise. "Well, you can move to Norway and live with Great-Aunt Inga, then," he said. "I still like summer. So there."

Kari climbed down from the stool. Kicking it away, she kneeled in the straw to scrub at the long white hair that grew down my legs and over my hooves, known by the humans as feathers.

"I bet you like winter better, too, don't you, Jingle?" Kari said. "There's less work for you in the fields. You get to rest unless you're driving us to town or church. And of course there are lots of extra carrots for Christmas. . . ."

I was half dozing as she picked the dirt out of my feathers. But I perked up as I heard that familiar word: *Christmas.*

Lars was passing by on his way to put the double tree away, and he heard the word, too. "It's a long time to Christmas, young ones," he said, pausing in front of my stall. "Or are you talking about how our Jingle Bells got his name?"

He reached in to give me a pat. Anders let out a groan.

"Don't encourage her, Papa!" he exclaimed. "She tells that story every chance she gets!"

"That's because it's a good story," Kari informed her brother.

Their father chuckled. "Indeed, it is. Kari always was a precocious thing—she was just three years old when we bought Jingle, who was much the same age at the time."

"I remember." Kari sat back on her heels, looking up at her father. "I was smaller then, but he was nearly as big as he is now!"

I stayed very still, not wanting to bump into her and hurt her. But hearing that human word—*Christmas*—had set my mind wandering as I thought back to my arrival on the farm. It was the first time I'd left the place where I was born. Until that day, I hadn't realized how big the world was. I had never really believed that there was anything beyond the green fields of my home and the dirt roads nearby where I'd been taught to drive, though my dam and the other adult horses had tried to tell me otherwise.

Then one day, my former master had tied me to the back of his carriage. I followed along behind it as I'd been taught. We proceeded at a trot down one road after another until we left everything familiar behind. Suddenly every tree, every cow, every stone in the road was strange. I eyed the new sights with suspicion.

*What is happening?* I'd called to the horse pulling the carriage, a burly Clydesdale gelding. *Will we ever stop?*

*I don't know,* the other horse had replied. *It's better not to wonder about the ways of humans.*

I hadn't been sure that was true at the time, though I understood it better now. Still, I'd tried to be good and behave as I'd been taught while my former master untied me and led me up a strange, new drive past a tidy, gabled frame house.

Lars and several of his children were waiting near the barn. Standing behind them was another horse, a stoutly built older mare. Everything looked new and strange, but it was good to see another horse, especially as we'd left the other Clydesdale out of sight by the road. I let out an anxious whinny to let the mare know I was there and willing to be friends. The mare snorted kindly in response. She was already hitched to the wagon, and almost before I knew what was happening, I was in the harness beside her.

*Steady, young one,* she told me in her wise, calm way. *These humans will treat you well if you work hard.*

*I can do that,* I said, though I still felt nervous. When the mare stepped forward, I did as well. I knew how to do this—my previous master had been training me to drive for quite some time already. The familiar feeling of the collar against my shoulders steadied me, and I threw myself into the work with relief.

Suddenly there came a peal of laughter. It startled me, and I jumped in place, causing the small silver bells on the harness to jingle loudly. It was Kari, much smaller then, grinning ear to ear.

"Jingle bells! Jingle bells!" she cried, running toward me.

"Kari, no!" Her mother, Frida, dashed forward.

But she was too slow. The tiny girl had flung her arms around my knee. I wasn't sure what to do, so I stood stock-still. A moment later, Frida pulled little Kari away.

Lars let out a long breath and smiled. "I think we've got a good one here," he said, giving me a pat on the neck. He turned to my former master. "What do you call him?"

The man shrugged. "Haven't really settled on a name," he said. "We just call him the tall colt, mostly."

Just then I shifted my weight, setting the bells jingling again.

"Jingle bells!" little Kari yelped with delight.

Lars raised an eyebrow. "Perhaps he's found his name already."

". . . and that's how our Jingle Bells got his name," Kari was saying now, smiling smugly at Anders.

Lars chuckled. "All right. I suppose Jonas and I had better go bring in the cows before the rain starts." He whistled for the dogs. They bounded after the two men, their excited barking fading into the distance and leaving the barn quiet and peaceful.

Kari finished her grooming and then brought me my dinner. The kitten came with her, leaping and pouncing in the hay after imaginary mice. I stepped carefully toward my feed bucket, watching where I placed my hooves. Kari leaned against my shoulder and hummed a pretty tune as I dipped my nose into the bucket. In the next stall, I could hear Millie slurping her grain.

Suddenly there was an excited cry from the barn door. It was Hanne, one of Kari's older sisters.

"A letter!" she cried, rushing in. "A letter has arrived from Martin!"

# The Letter

"From Martin?" Kari exclaimed. "What does it say?"

Anders rushed in from the direction of the tack room. "Did it come all the way from Detroit?" he added, sounding excited.

"Where do you think it came from?" Hanne

retorted in her tart way. "That's where he and Pearl live, isn't it? Now, where's Papa?"

"He and Jonas just left to bring the cows in for milking," Anders said. "I suppose he can see the letter when he comes in for supper later."

"No! There's big news," Hanne said. "Mama wants him to see it right away."

Hearing the urgency in the older girl's voice, I pulled my nose out of the bucket, though I continued chewing steadily. The name Hanne had mentioned—Martin—was one I knew. It was the name of the family's eldest son, who had left the farm several years earlier. At first I'd thought he was gone forever, much like the old mare, who had died at around the same time Martin had gone away.

But one day the following year Martin had returned for a visit, bringing a young woman with him. The woman had a soft, quick voice, pale skin, dark hair, and very red lips. When Martin showed her around the barnyard, she'd seemed rather fearful of Millie and me, though I didn't understand why, especially since Millie had pulled her home in the family's small buggy earlier that very day.

Kari stepped forward. "I'll fetch Papa," she told Hanne. "Jingle can take me to find him."

Anders frowned. "Poor Jingle just worked all day in the hot sun. I'm sure he'd rather finish his dinner. And Papa will be back soon."

But Kari was already reaching for my halter. I lowered my head and allowed her to lead me out of the stall.

"It's all right," she told her brother. "Jingle doesn't mind, do you, boy? Now, help me up."

Anders shrugged and stepped forward. He wove his fingers together into a step for Kari, tossing her lightly up and onto my broad back. She scrabbled into position, holding on to my mane until she found her balance.

"Be careful, Kari." Hanne seemed anxious, like Millie when the dogs started barking at coyotes in the woods beyond the pasture. "Are you sure Anders shouldn't go instead?"

"Don't be a simp. I'm fine," Kari assured her sister. "Jingle always takes care of me."

Anders clipped a length of rope to the halter and led me outside. Then he tossed his end of the rope to Kari. I'd been ridden this way many times. The rider tugged on the rope to tell me which way he or she wanted to go. That sort of thing worked well when I was in harness, with

Lars behind me holding the long reins that ran over my back to the bridle. However, I wished I could have told Kari that her rope rein wasn't really necessary. I could always tell which way she wanted me to go by feeling her weight shift on my back.

"Sorry to take you away from your supper, Jingle." I felt her tiny hand rub my withers as we walked across the barnyard. "Silly Hanne gets excited about the strangest things or nothing at all, but if Mama is so eager for Papa to see that letter, there must be something important in it." She let out a gasp. "Oh! Do you suppose Martin is coming back here to live? No, that couldn't be it—he loves his job. He says the Ford Motor Company is the best place in the world to work. . . ."

She continued chattering in the same vein. I paid little attention to the words, though I liked the musical lilt of her voice. It was easy to guess what she was feeling by the type of tune it carried. Today it was lively and irregular, skittering like the kitten chasing a bug over a log.

We headed down the hill, following the dirt track leading between the hay fields and the cattle pasture. I could feel the slight shift in Kari's weight as she lifted an arm to shade her eyes against the sun hanging low in the afternoon sky.

"I don't see them or the herd, either," she said. "They must be at the far end of the pasture. Come on, let's hurry!"

Her skinny legs thumped against my sides. I spent more time in harness than being ridden, and it took me a moment to work out what she was asking. She wanted me to go faster.

My body was weary after the day's work, but I lumbered into a trot. Kari clucked and squeezed my sides again. "Faster, Jingle," she said. "Good boy!"

I spotted Lars and Jonas before Kari did. The two men were bending over one of the dairy cows. She lay flat on the ground, her sides heaving. The dogs were circling around, seeming agitated. The rest of the herd was grazing nearby.

After a moment, Kari noticed the group, too. "Oh! Did Hazel have her calf?" she exclaimed. "Hurry, Jingle!"

I trotted steadily on. Lars looked up as he heard me coming. His pale brows were drawn into an expression of worry.

"Kari!" he said. "What are you— Never mind. I'm glad you're here. We need to get this calf back to the barn—it came early and needs attention."

"Jingle can carry it!" Kari said.

"Good idea," Jonas said. He leaned over the calf, which I could see more clearly now, lying still behind its mother. "Come, Papa. I'll help you lift it onto his back."

"Wait." Lars stopped his son with a hand on the shoulder. "Let Jingle smell it first. We don't want to spook him."

"Jingle?" Kari laughed. "He never spooks at anything."

"True enough." Lars smiled, reaching for my halter. "He's as steady as they come. Still, let him have a look first."

He led me forward a few steps. The cow grunted and rolled into an upright position. *My baby, my baby!* she lowed anxiously.

There was nothing strange to me about a calf—several were born on the farm every year, and Millie and I grazed among them nearly every day. I also saw nothing alarming about the men hoisting the calf between them.

They carried it past my head and lifted it higher. I raised my head and rolled back my eyes. Now what were they doing?

"Good boy, Jingle," Kari said, reaching down toward the calf. "Steady, boy."

A moment later, I felt the calf's twitchy, sticky weight settle over my withers, resting just in front of Kari. The creature's legs hung down on either side of me, the tiny hooves moving weakly against my shoulders. It felt odd, and for a moment I laid my ears back in consternation.

Then I felt Kari patting me and heard Lars speaking my name, and the moment of worry passed. I could smell the calf and feel Kari's legs against my sides. This was no different from the times the humans had used my strength to transport sacks of potatoes or freshly cured cheeses, which meant it was nothing to worry about after all. Just another job to do.

"Good man." Lars patted my neck and took my lead rope from his daughter. "Come now, we'll take it slow and steady."

"That's just the way Jingle likes it," Kari said with a laugh.

We started out. Once or twice I felt the calf slip, and stopped long enough for Kari and her father to move it back into position. The whole way back to the barn I could hear the anxious cow mooing along behind me with Jonas at her

head, but I paid her little mind. Even the dogs seemed to sense that we were on important business and trotted along with minimal barking or silliness.

Anders and Hanne were waiting for us outside the barn. "What took you so long?" Hanne complained, shading her eyes to peer at us. Then she saw the calf and her expression changed. "Oh! What happened?"

There was a flurry of human talk that I didn't try to follow. Hanne kited off toward the house as quickly as a dog after a rabbit, returning moments later with her mother and a pail of hot water. In the meantime, Lars and Anders had lifted the calf down carefully and laid it in the pile of hay sweepings near the barn door. Jonas tied its anxious mother nearby.

Kari slid down from my back and fetched a rag and a stiff brush to clean off my withers and sides where the sticky calf had lain. But she paused often to watch as the others worked over the calf. Hanne and her mother were watching, too. I glanced toward the stall where the rest of my supper waited, but nobody seemed to remember that except me. So I cocked a hoof and dozed as Kari groomed me.

Finally Lars backed away from the calf, smiling. "I think she'll be all right," he said. "We found her in time."

"Thank goodness!" Frida clasped her hands.

Hanne tugged on her sleeve. "Mama, the letter."

"Oh! I'd nearly forgotten in all the excitement." Frida reached into her apron pocket and pulled out a scrap of paper. "Lars, you'll never believe Martin's news!"

"Another letter from Martin?" Lars wiped his hands on a rag, sounding surprised. "Didn't we have one just last week?"

"Yes," Anders said, rolling his eyes. "He couldn't stop bragging about his wonderful job at the Ford Motor Company and his wonderful life in the big city."

"Hush, Anders," Frida chided. "As I said, Martin has big news that couldn't wait. Here!" She shoved the letter toward her husband.

Lars smiled and held up a hand. "You know I'm not much for reading, my dearest. Puzzling through a letter would take me all night, and there's still the herd to bring in and the milking to do. Why don't you read it to all of us?"

"Very well." Frida cleared her throat and looked at the paper.

*Greetings from Detroit, family!*

*I trust you are all well. I know you probably weren't expecting another letter from me so soon, but our news couldn't wait. My beloved bride, Pearl, just found out she's expecting a baby. It's due to arrive a month before Christmas! I'll telephone soon with more details.*

*Yours faithfully,*
*Martin*

The family erupted into a tempest of exclamations. The dogs, sensing the excitement, leaped and barked and twisted themselves nearly inside out. Kari dropped her grooming tools and rushed to her mother, insisting on examining the letter herself. Finding myself free, I took a step toward my stall, and then another. I could smell the remainder of my dinner still awaiting me in its bucket. However, the newborn calf lay between me and my stall, and I stopped short, trying to work out a way around it. That was when Lars finally noticed me.

"Ah, Jingle!" he said. "Kari, don't just leave the horse standing loose—he could decide to wander off and leave us, and then how would we manage the plowing?"

"Oh, Papa," Kari said with a laugh. "Jingle would never leave us!"

She grabbed the dangling lead rope and took me around the calf and into my stall. There, I settled into enjoying my feed as the humans rushed off toward the house.

# An October Sunday

The long, hot days of summer faded into the shorter, crisper ones of autumn. Before long, the trees were dropping their colorful leaves, and the nights left frost on the pastures. However, Millie and I grew plush winter coats to keep the cold at bay, and our flexible lips easily pushed the leaves aside so we could nibble the frost-nipped grass. The cows still produced milk, of course, and Millie and I were needed to haul the heavy silver cans to the local cheese maker. We also took turns pulling the family carriage and buggy to town for church, shopping, and visiting. But the hay and corn had been harvested, which meant less work for horse and human alike.

One mild, bright autumn day it was my turn to pull the family to church. Kari always gave me an extra-careful brushing on church days, and Anders polished the metal parts of the harness to a shine. The entire family piled into the carriage, and we set out on the easy five-mile journey into town.

When we arrived, several familiar horses were already tied to the hitching rail in front of the clapboard church. The family climbed out and joined the groups of humans heading inside, though Jonas lingered just long enough to lead me over and tie me beside a friendly Belgian draft mare known as Dolly.

*What a fine day, Jingle,* she greeted me as Jonas hurried away after the others.

*Indeed. The grass is short in my pasture, but it still tastes fine,* I replied, cocking a hind foot.

Beyond Dolly's carriage stood an elegant hackney gelding named Star. *You still have grass?* he said. *My master's sheep have eaten our pasture down to the roots!*

Dolly let out a snort. *Sheep are annoying beasts,* she began. *They—*

A sudden loud honk cut her off and made us all jump. It sounded as if a giant goose had just cried out behind us. Star startled so dramatically that his harness jingled.

*What was that?* he exclaimed, showing the whites of his eyes as he tried to see past the buggy behind him.

*You should recognize the sound by now, Dolly* replied. *The humans call it a horseless carriage.*

I flicked an ear back as I heard the thing rattle by with its strange growling sound. Over the past few years, I'd shared the roads more and more

often with these so-called horseless carriages. I didn't understand how their wheels rolled with neither horse nor mule to pull them, but I figured it was another mystery of humans.

*It's gone now, in any case,* I said. *Besides, such matters are nothing to worry about.*

*Don't be too sure.* This comment came from a horse farther down the line, a lanky chestnut gelding whose name I didn't know. *I pulled a merchant's cart in a larger town until recently, where there are many more horseless carriages than you have here. I once saw one run straight into a wagon like a fox into a flock of chickens! The horse pulling it was knocked to the ground and nearly broke his leg!*

*Well, that doesn't happen here,* Dolly told the newcomer.

*Indeed,* I put in. *We have only a few horseless*

*carriages here, and they show little interest in mingling with us.*

After that, talk returned to more interesting topics—grass and rain and soft, sweet hay. Eventually the warm sun on our backs made us sleepy, and our talk drifted away with the cool breeze that served as the day's only hint that winter's chill would soon be upon us.

I was dozing when the family emerged from the church building some time later. Kari raced over to untie me, while the others followed more slowly. Hanne and the eldest sister, Asta, had stopped to talk to some other girls their age, all of them dressed in colorful skirts and hats.

Star's master walked past with his wife. He was a stout man with a booming voice and a nose the color of a rooster's comb.

"Good day, Lars," he said with a tip of his hat. "Your big Clydesdale looks especially handsome today. Just remember to call me first if you ever wish to sell him." He grinned broadly and winked.

"Jingle isn't for sale, sir!" Kari said.

The man chuckled along with the other adults. "I'm afraid my daughter is right, Arthur," Lars said. "He's not for sale."

"But thank you for the compliment, Arthur," Frida added. "Your Star is a fine animal as well."

Arthur smiled and gave a little bow in her direction. "And how is your eldest these days, madam?" he asked. "Still down in Detroit working for Mr. Ford, eh?"

"He is doing very well, thank you," Frida replied. "He says the factory is having trouble keeping up with the demand for the automobiles they're building."

Anders stepped forward. "Martin thinks that someday everyone will get around in Mr. Ford's Model T automobile. What do you think about that?"

"Hmm. We shall see." Arthur sounded skeptical. He stepped closer and ran a hand down my neck. "Who wants to ride in a noisy bit of tin when one could sit behind a fine animal such as this?"

"And what of the baby?" Arthur's wife spoke up eagerly. "Have you heard any news, Frida?"

"Not lately—but Pearl isn't due for several weeks yet," Frida replied.

"I see." Arthur's wife smiled. "So it could be a Christmas baby!"

Kari grinned. "If it is, maybe they could name

it Jingle Bells!" she exclaimed. She rubbed my nose as the others laughed. "You wouldn't mind sharing your name, would you, boy?"

"I hope the baby comes well before *Jul*," Frida said. "Pearl is already nervous about taking a baby on such a long train journey. If the baby comes too close to Christmas, she might think it's simply too young, and Martin might not be able to come home for the holiday!"

"Oh, dear." Arthur's wife clucked sympathetically.

The humans continued to chat, but I was focused on Kari. She'd just reached into her skirts and pulled out half a cookie, which she held beneath my muzzle on her upturned hand. I lipped it off her palm eagerly, ignoring the curious looks from the other horses.

When we arrived back at the farm, Lars unhitched me, humming all the while. By the time he finished, Kari had emerged from the house. Her church dress had disappeared, replaced by her everyday clothes.

"What do you need me to do, Papa?" she asked.

"Nothing at the moment, child." Lars tousled her butter-colored hair. "We won't have many more fine, sunny days like this one before the snow starts falling. Go out and have fun—just be back in time to help with the milking, all right?"

"I promise!" Kari said. "May I take Jingle for a ride? I know a place where he can graze—I don't think even the deer have found it."

Her father smiled. "He'll enjoy that."

Soon Kari was on my bare back, lead rope

in hand. She guided me out of the barnyard and through the patch of trees on the far side of the house. The sun was almost too warm on my plush coat, making me feel drowsy. But I walked steadily in the direction she guided me. After a little while, we came to a large, grassy clearing with a stream trickling through it.

"There you go, Jingle." Kari loosened the rope. "It's all for you!"

I lowered my head eagerly and grazed. The grass was much longer than that in the pasture and still tasted faintly of summer. Kari swung her legs up, resting her feet on my withers and her head on my broad rump. She'd done the same many times before, staring up at the sky as I grazed.

"Did you ever wonder why the clouds take the shapes they do, Jingle?" she mused. "There's one

over there that looks just like one of Papa's work boots. And, oh! Here comes one that looks like a horse. Maybe it's old Nell, come back to visit us. . . ."

I flicked an ear briefly at the name, though for a moment I wasn't sure why it sounded familiar. Then I remembered. Nell had been the name of the family's wise old mare, the one they'd had when I arrived. For a moment I paused, remembering the scent of her and her honest way of leaning into the harness beside me. But soon the grass called to me, and I returned to grazing.

Kari talked a little more, though I was too focused on the grass to pay the words much mind. Eventually her voice drifted off. I felt her breathing slow and deepen and knew she was asleep.

After that, I was extra careful not to jostle her as I stepped from one patch of grass to the next. The sun arced across the sky, and the only sounds were the birds and the trickle of the stream and Kari's soft breaths. I was content.

I'd just savored a bite of delectable clover when I heard a shout. Kari heard it, too. It was Anders, riding toward us bareback on Millie.

"There you are!" he cried as Kari scrambled back into a sitting position. "Papa and Jonas just went to bring the cows in. You'd better come home, or you'll be in trouble."

Kari glanced at the sun, now sinking toward the horizon. "I must have fallen asleep," she said with a yawn. "Thanks for coming to get me."

"You're welcome. But we'd better hurry, or we'll *both* be in trouble." Anders squinted at the sun, then grinned at his sister. "I know—let's race back to the barn."

"Race?" Kari sounded dubious.

"Last one back has to take the other's turn cleaning out the chicken coop!" Anders shouted, digging his heels into Millie's sides.

The mare flattened her ears and humped her back. I expected her to buck, but she didn't. After one more kick from Anders, she picked up a grudging trot.

"Come on, Jingle," Kari said with a laugh. "We can catch them at that rate!"

She clucked and gave me a nudge with her heels. I was full and a bit sleepy from the afternoon's grazing and would just as soon have stopped for a nap in the shade. But I could tell what Kari wanted, so I broke into a trot. When she nudged again, I lumbered into a canter.

Anders glanced back as he heard us coming. "Let's go, Millie, you lazy beast!" he cried, once again thumping the mare's sides with both legs.

This time Millie responded at once, bursting into a gallop. Within seconds she left us behind, disappearing beyond the next grove of trees.

"Ho, Jingle." Kari gave a tug on the lead rope and leaned back.

I slowed to a trot, then a walk. Kari leaned forward and patted my neck.

"It's all right, boy," she said. I could feel the smile in her body. "You might not be the fastest horse in Wisconsin, but I don't mind. You're still the best."

# News

Several more days passed in the usual manner. I pulled a heavy load of milk to the cheese maker's farm down the road. Millie took Frida and Asta to town to do the shopping. The cows came in twice a day for milking. It remained warm for the season, and the grass was still green.

Then one morning, something different happened. I was in my stall savoring the last bites of my breakfast. Millie was snuffling at the partition between us; she had already finished her ration and was eyeing mine. A pair of hens was picking around beneath my bucket for dropped bits of grain, and the kitten—almost a cat now—was watching them from the doorway, her tail twitching, though she knew better than to pounce on the feisty hens.

Out in the barn, Lars, Jonas, and Anders had just finished the milking. Kari was scrubbing buckets, and Hanne had come out to feed the family's breakfast scraps to the chickens. The dogs were milling around, hoping for a taste of milk or some other attention. The whole barn felt busy and warm and pleasant.

Suddenly the door flew open, letting in a blast of chilly air. Frida and Asta rushed in.

"She's here!" Frida cried. "The baby is here! Martin just telephoned!"

"What?" Kari dropped the bucket she was holding with a clatter that made the cat jump, hiss, and run off. "The baby—it's here already?"

Excitement swirled through the barn, making the air feel different. The dogs leaped and barked around the humans. I left the last bite of grain in my bucket and stepped to the stall door to look out. To my left, I saw Millie doing the same.

"Yes, Martin just called," Asta said, her voice dancing with elation. "The baby came earlier than the doctor was expecting, but everything is all right. She's healthy, and her name is Eva. Isn't that pretty?"

"Pearl is well, too," Frida added. "Martin says it was an easy birth."

"Oh, praise be!" Lars clasped his hands before him. "We have a granddaughter, Frida my dearest!"

Lars and Frida embraced, while children and dogs danced around them, filling the air with joyful sounds. Millie was still watching, wide-eyed and with flared nostrils.

*What is it?* she wondered. *Is something going to happen?*

*They're happy,* I replied. *It's nothing for us to worry about.* I stepped back over to clean out the bottom of my bucket.

By the time I finished, my stall door was swinging open. Kari stood there, her eyes brighter than ever.

"Come, Jingle!" she exclaimed. "We've got to get over to Morfar and Mormor's house. They'll want to hear the news right away!"

Anders appeared behind her, a lead rope in his hand. "I don't know why they won't just install a telephone," he complained. "That way they could have the news already. They're so old-fashioned!"

"Never mind." Kari grabbed the rope from him and clipped it to my halter. "Help me get Jingle ready, please?"

Soon I was hitched to the carriage. Nearly the entire family piled in, leaving only Jonas behind to put the cows back out to pasture with the help of the dogs.

"Step lively, Jingle," Lars ordered as we headed out onto the road. "We have important news to share!"

As soon as we'd made two turns, I knew where we were going. Frida's mother and father lived in a tiny town about a dozen miles from the farm. The family went there often to visit, and I knew the way well. It involved several twisting, winding roads leading to a much larger paved road that ran through a number of larger towns. I always met numerous other carriages and wagons going in either direction, of every type from the smallest pony traps to humble farm wagons to the large, heavy public stagecoaches pulled by a team. It was a common thing to meet horseless carriages as well.

That day was no exception. As we turned onto the larger road, there was a sudden roar. A horseless carriage burst into view over the rise, rushing toward us like a black growling wolf.

"Ho, Jingle! Easy," Lars called, tightening his hold on the reins.

I had already stopped short, not wishing to tangle with the horseless carriage. My heart pounded as it raced past, the mere width of a horse's head from my muzzle, its strange sound and smell filling my mind. The human inside lifted a hand in a jaunty wave, and that loud, gooselike sound emanated from the thing as it disappeared ahead of us.

"That was close!" Hanne exclaimed, her voice shaky.

"Indeed." Lars sounded disapproving. "Those things are becoming a menace on the roads lately."

He flicked the reins upon my back and asked me to walk on. I took a cautious step forward, but only after looking to the side to make sure there were no more of those honking, growling horseless carriages coming. There were not, and the voice of my master behind me reminded me that I had a job to do.

I picked up a steady trot, ignoring the other carriages that passed. After a few minutes, I again heard that unsettling growling, this time up ahead. It was a horseless carriage—a different one this time, with a man and woman seated within. I kept my head up and focused on it. But I soon saw that this horseless carriage was moving at a more reasonable speed than the other and lowered my head to its usual position. Still, I kept a careful eye on the growling beast until it had passed us and moved out of sight.

After a while, we turned off the main road

onto a smaller lane and soon reached a familiar log house. Mormor Johanne was outside sweeping the porch when Lars steered me into the small yard. She dropped her broom and rushed forward when she saw us.

"Oh, what a surprise!" she cried with delight, pausing to rub my nose as she passed me on the way to the carriage. "Hello, Jingle Bells," she said. "Where are your bells today?"

Kari had already hopped out of the carriage. "Oh, Mormor," she said with a laugh. "Jingle only wears his bells at Christmas!"

"True," Frida said. "But perhaps we should have put them on today." She climbed out behind her daughter. "It *is* a special occasion. . . ."

The humans swirled around one another with hugs and cries and news. After a moment, Morfar came outside, leaning on his cane, and added his voice to the others.

I had stopped listening by then, however. Mormor and Morfar's buggy horse, a pretty liver chestnut known as Queenie, had come into view in her small paddock beside the house.

*Jingle!* she said. *It has been a goat's age since I've seen you!*

I snorted a greeting in return, which made Lars remember to tie me at the fence. After that, the humans went inside, though Mormor reemerged just long enough to feed me several crunchy, sweet carrots.

"Don't worry, Jingle," she said, running her gnarled hand over my face. "Even in all the excitement, I didn't forget your favorite treat."

I nuzzled her gratefully. Mormor fed a carrot

to Queenie over the fence before heading back
inside.

Queenie and I traded our own news of grass
and rest and work. After a while, we heard the
jingling of a harness coming closer.

*Who's that?* I asked, seeing a small buggy

pulled by a narrow-built dapple-gray horse turning into the yard.

*It's Pepper,* Queenie said. *His mistress often vis-
its with mine.*

A stout older woman was driving. "Oh, dear,"
she said, eyeing me as she climbed out of the
buggy. "What a large horse! I hope you'll have
enough space to wait while I gossip with Johanne,
Pepper."

She tittered to herself as she tied her horse
beside me. Humming under her breath, she hurried away into the house. Pepper eyed me curi-
ously, and soon we were acquainted.

*Is your carriage very heavy?* Pepper asked me.
*It's quite large.*

*Not too heavy,* I responded. *My harness mate,*

Millie, *complains of it, but it gives me no more trouble than a plow in rough ground.*

Pepper didn't respond. He was rolling his eyes away from me, toward the road, and his head had gone up.

A moment later, the sound he'd heard reached my ears—a now-familiar growl. Soon the horseless carriage raced past us, kicking up gravel and dust and blowing it toward us as it passed. The yard was very small, and it sounded as if the thing might run right into our carriages.

Pepper immediately started dancing in place, shaking the traces and making his harness jingle. *No, no, no, no!* he cried. *It's too much; it's too close; it's too loud.*

*Easy, friend,* Queenie said. *It's just one of those*

*odd human contraptions. You must have passed them on the road many times.*

*I have, but I still don't like them sneaking up behind me!* Pepper's eyes rolled back toward me. *Don't you find them terrifying? How can you just stand there with such monsters rushing by?*

*How can I not?* I replied, cocking an ear after the sound of the horseless carriage, which was already fading into the distance. *I would prefer not to waste energy on such worries when I know I could better use it for work.*

That seemed to settle Pepper's mind a little, and the three of us returned to chatting to pass the time until our humans needed us again.

# Christmas Hunting

We animals paid little attention to human holidays, except that they sometimes meant a day off from the hay wagon or the plow, and perhaps an apple or other treat in our ration. But I always noticed *Lussinatten*, when we animals got extra feed in our buckets. That day also meant that

Christmas was approaching. I didn't know why Christmas was so important to the humans; I only understood that it had something to do with my name, and that the silver bells would soon be chiming from my harness.

Christmas also meant some unusual behavior from the humans. One chilly but still morning, Kari came to fetch me right after milking. Her eyes were as bright as ever, and her small body quivered with excitement. She had a burlap sack in one hand, and for a moment I hoped she had brought me carrot tops or apple peelings from the house as she sometimes did. But the bag appeared to be empty, with no scent of any such treats, and I quickly lost interest.

"I need your help, Jingle," Kari said as she opened my stall door. One of the dogs, a lively little terrier the humans called Dash, was at her heels, though the others were still out helping return the cows to their pasture.

I pricked my ears toward Kari and lowered my head. She grabbed my halter and led me out.

*Where are you going?* Millie called. *Aren't we going out to pasture?*

*I don't know,* I replied, careful not to step on Kari's heels as I followed her outside. Dash trotted along beside me, his pink tongue hanging out nearly to the ground. He was the boldest of the dogs, never seeming to notice or care that one of my hooves was nearly as large as his entire body.

Soon Kari was clambering nimbly onto my back from the stone wall outside the barn. She draped her burlap sack over my withers, and her legs and the rope on my halter guided me across the road and into a field that had grown tall with corn over the summer but was now nothing but rough, frostbitten stubble. Beyond lay the pine forest where Lars and Jonas sometimes took the wagon to gather kindling.

I maintained a steady, unhurried walk across the field, being careful to avoid soft spots. Dash raced in circles around me, his stubby tail wagging nonstop.

*Adventure! Adventure!* he barked.

"Hush, Dash!" Kari scolded, and I could feel her turn her head to look back the way we'd come. "I don't want Hanne to see where we're going and steal my idea. You see, Jingle, we're on a very important mission. I need to find some perfect pinecones and maybe some dried berries if the birds have left any." She lowered her voice, leaning forward to whisper in the direction of my ears. "I'm going to make them into a wreath for

baby Eva's crib. It will be her *Jul* gift from you and me, Jingle. Won't that be nice?"

Just then Dash barked and leaped forward, chasing a rabbit until it disappeared into a patch of weeds. Kari whistled to call him off, and the dog raced ahead toward the edge of the field, where the pines grew tall and straight like giant fence posts.

Soon Kari and I were following a dirt trail into the forest. There was little underbrush beneath the deep shade of the pines, and it was easy to see a good distance in every direction. Even a skittish horse like Pepper wouldn't have any reason to be nervous.

"Ho, Jingle," Kari said, squeezing with her thighs.

I stopped obediently, casting an eye back

toward her. She leaned to the side, hanging on to a chunk of my mane to keep her aboard. She plucked a pinecone off a nearby branch and examined it.

"Too small," she said after a moment. "Papa says the tallest trees are in the middle of the forest. Those should have bigger cones."

She tossed the pinecone aside. Dash saw it fall and raced over, grabbing it and worrying it like the kitten with a mouse. Kari ignored the dog, nudging me forward.

It was pleasant in the wood. The trees blocked the wind, which had been growing colder every day, though there had been little snow so far. Birds flitted in the treetops, and small creatures rustled here and there, attracting Dash's attention. Kari hummed as she rode, her body warm and completely relaxed on my back.

I was relaxed, too. But I still kept an eye out for hazards, stepping carefully over roots and fallen branches and avoiding the occasional hole or loose bit of stone. Two or three times Kari stopped me to grab another pinecone but tossed them all aside as well.

Eventually we reached a small clearing. The sun peeking through allowed brush to thrive here—I had to step around a tangle of brambles, and then found the path blocked by a wild grape-vine stretching from one tree trunk to the next.

"Wait, Jingle!" Kari exclaimed. "That vine is perfect for my wreath!"

She threw one leg over me and slid to the ground, slowing her descent by hanging on to my mane as long as possible. She landed as softly as a bird, then scampered over to grab the grapevine.

Dash trotted over, too, sniffing the vine with interest.

Kari pulled a small pocketknife out of her clothes and started sawing at the vine. Soon she had several long, twisty strands in her hand. She shoved them into her bag. Dash grabbed the cut end of one of the vines and gave it a yank. It came loose and coiled around him, causing the little dog to leap back in surprise.

Kari nearly fell over with laughter. "That's what you get, treating everything like a rat to be killed," she told Dash fondly. "Oh! But you've given me an idea. . . ."

She dropped her bag and cut another long strand of vine, which she wove into a large loop. Using some string from her pocket, she tied several pinecones onto it. When she was finished, she gave a light tug on my lead rope. I lowered my head, and she slid the loop of vine right over so that it settled around my neck like my work collar. It felt a little strange, like large flies pricking at me. My skin shuddered a bit, but I stayed still.

"Perfect!" Kari exclaimed, clapping her hands. "See, Jingle? It's a special Christmas necklace for you! We can pretend that the pinecones are jingle bells, and that we're dashing through the snow to Mormor's house. I can't wait until we do that for real on Christmas Eve! I know baby Eva will love to hear you jingling along!"

She started humming again, then burst into song:

*"Dashing through the snow*
*In a one-horse open sleigh . . ."*

There was more, but the words meant little to me. I let my eyes fall half-shut, enjoying the sound of her voice, as sweet as any birdsong.

Soon Dash started barking again. *Noise! Noise!* he cried, spinning in a circle. That made Kari break off her song with a laugh.

"I suppose we'd better keep going," she said. "I still need to find some good cones for my wreath."

She tossed the bag onto my rump and used a jagged tree stump to climb back up. With a nudge from her heels, we continued across the clearing and back into the shade. We wandered awhile longer, until finally Kari let out a cry.

"Look! That's the biggest pinecone I've ever seen!" she exclaimed. "Over there, Jingle!"

She tugged at the rope, guiding me to the

base of an especially large tree. Then she pulled her legs up, bringing them beneath her. I could feel both of her tiny feet against me as she carefully stood up on my broad, flat back.

"Stand still, Jingle," she said. "I think I can reach it if I stretch—"

At that moment, a squirrel burst out from beneath a fallen log and made a mad run for the large tree. Dash had been sniffing around nearby but instantly gave chase, barking wildly. He raced after the squirrel, passing between my front legs and beneath my belly before veering to the side.

"Oh!" Kari cried, startled.

I was startled, too. But I never forgot the girl standing precariously upon my back and remained stock-still. Soon the squirrel was safely

up the tree, and Dash was left barking in frustration at the base.

"Naughty dog," Kari scolded, folding her legs and returning to her normal position on my back. "You nearly made me fall off in surprise. But never mind—I got my pinecone. And I think I see more big ones over there!"

Before long her sack was stuffed full, and we turned toward home. Kari had lost track of our path by then, but she wasn't worried. She knew that a horse can always find his way home, so she gave me my head.

As we emerged from the tree line some time later, we discovered that a soft snow had begun falling while we were beneath the shelter of the thick pine boughs. Already a light coating lay over the corn stubble.

"Snow!" Kari cried, and I could feel her tilt her head up toward the sky. "I hope it lasts more than a day this time before the sunshine burns it away. It won't seem like Christmas if we don't have snow!" She laughed. "Oh, but what am I saying? Martin and his family are coming home! Snow or no snow, this is sure to be the best Christmas since the very first one I remember." I felt her small hand pat my neck, then rattle the vine necklace around it. "That's the Christmas when I gave you your name, Jingle Bells."

After that, she sang all the rest of the way home.

## Martin's Mystery

Another week passed. In the meantime more snow came, enough to leave icicles in my feathers when Kari or her father or brothers walked me out to the pasture. The nights were cold, but most of the days were sunny and warm enough to melt away bits of the snow cover.

One chilly morning, I was dozing in my stall waiting for breakfast when Kari and Anders burst in. They were chattering excitedly, and after a moment Anders shouted with laughter at something his sister said, causing the dogs to start barking.

Millie came awake in her stall. *What is it?* she snorted. *What's wrong?*

I didn't respond, stepping to the front of my stall. Just then Lars entered the barn, followed by his wife.

"Kari, back inside!" Frida ordered. "I need your help with the baking."

"But, Mama, I want to give Jingle a good grooming," Kari protested, racing over to rub my nose. "I want him to look his best when baby Eva sees him for the first time."

Anders let out a huff. "As if a baby cares how well a horse is groomed!"

Kari ignored him. "May I please drive the carriage when we go into town to pick up Martin and Pearl and Eva?" she asked. "I know the way to the train station."

Lars and Frida traded a look. "Martin called to say nobody will need to pick them up," Lars told his daughter.

"What?" Anders glanced up from filling the chickens' feed pan. "Then how will they get here? It's a long walk from town."

"*Too* long in this weather, and with a baby," Kari added. I pricked my ears at the sound of distress in her voice. "Do you think they intend to rent a carriage?"

"I hope not," Lars said. "With Christmas so close, there are few available."

"I hope Martin realizes that," Frida said. "He's accustomed to Detroit's big-city ways these days, I suppose."

Her husband shrugged. "I don't know what he's thinking. We'll have to wait and see what happens."

Kari stepped over to the harness bells, which she'd hung on a hook near my stall the day before. They were covered in dust and cobwebs but still gleamed faintly against their long leather strap. When she touched them, they tinkled softly.

"May I polish the bells before I help with the baking?" Kari asked. "Please, Mama? I promise it won't take long. I want everything to be ready for our trip to Mormor and Morfar's house on Christmas Eve, and there won't be much time for such things once Martin arrives."

Frida smiled. "I suppose that would be all right. Hanne and Asta are probably all I need for the moment."

Kari helped her father feed Millie and me our morning grain. After that she sat down on a straw bale with the bells on her lap and a cloth in her hand. By the time her father and brothers finished the milking, the bells sparkled in the beams of sunlight coming in through the narrow windows.

"There," she said, holding up the strap to show me her work. "Now the bells are all ready for Christmas."

I nosed at the bells, setting them jingling

again. Kari giggled and shook them to make them jingle even more.

Her father glanced over. "Finished, Kari?" he said. "Good. Run along and help your mother. There's a lot to do before Martin arrives."

I spent the next few hours in the pasture. Millie took turns nibbling at the large hay bale Lars and Jonas had put out for us and digging for grass beneath the snow. The cows and I focused mostly on the hay, which returned more food for less effort. Once my belly was full, I cocked a hind foot and let my eyes drift shut. The sun felt warm on my back, and I was soon asleep.

Sometime later, Kari's familiar whistle woke me. She climbed into the pasture and hurried closer as I ambled to meet her.

"The house is spotless, the baking is finished, and the stockings are by the fire," she declared breathlessly. "I had to get out of the house before Mama decided to start the cleaning all over again! Come, Jingle, Papa said I can take you to graze in the front yard—there's not much snow left there where the sun beats down, and plenty of grass."

I pricked my ears at the word *grass* and lowered my head so she could clip on the lead rope. She led me to the little patch of ground between the house and the road. Most of the snow there had melted away, and I lowered my head to graze, savoring the taste of the moist grass—so different from the dry hay I'd been eating all day.

As we wandered around the yard, several carriages passed on the road nearby. Once I lifted my head to greet Dolly as she trotted slowly along in front of her master's carriage. But mostly I focused on my food.

Then I heard the sound of a horseless carriage coming. I was standing close to the road and lifted my head, a little wary still of the strange creatures. To my surprise, the horseless carriage slowed and turned into the drive beside the house.

Kari let out a gasp. "Martin?" she cried. "Is it you?"

I recognized him now, too. Kari's eldest brother shared her light hair and eyes, though his skin was paler and his clothes looked different. The young woman who had come with him last time was seated beside him, cradling a swaddled baby in her arms.

"Merry Christmas, Kari!" Martin cried, cutting off the growling sound of his carriage and jumping out. "We're here! Do you like my surprise?"

He leaned back in and did something with his hand, which caused that gooselike sound: *aWOOOga!*

I jumped and laid my ears back, startled to hear the sound so close by and sudden. Kari glanced up at me, then back at her brother. "Your surprise? What is it?"

Martin grinned. "Come on, little sister. This farm isn't that far from civilization, is it? I'm sure we passed a few other automobiles on our way here. It's a Model T Ford! My Model T Ford, to be precise."

By now the rest of the family was pouring out of the house. "This automobile belongs to you, son?" Lars exclaimed. "But how can you afford such a luxury?"

"A Model T isn't a luxury anymore, Papa." Martin patted the hood of the thing, causing a hollow clunk that made my ears prick forward again. "Mr. Ford has created a new way of building motorcars so that more people can afford them. I bought this one with just four months' pay!"

"Boy, that's something!" Anders was circling the motorcar, his eyes wide. "Can I drive it, Martin?"

"Never mind that." Frida pushed past the others to reach the horseless carriage. "Welcome, Pearl. And this must be little Eva. . . ."

The family gathered around the horseless carriage. The young woman climbed out of the car, and the baby was handed from Frida to Lars to Asta to Hanne. Jonas and Anders hung back, laughing nervously as the baby squalled. Only Kari was left out of the group, since she was still holding my lead rope.

Finally Martin noticed his youngest sister hanging back. He stepped over to us. "Hello, Jingle," he said, giving me a pat. "I hope you're not too concerned about my Model T. But I wouldn't

blame you a bit if you were. Thanks to the Ford Motor Company, horses won't be needed at all soon enough, and you'll be out of a job!"

Kari frowned. "Don't be silly, Martin," she said. "Come, Jingle. I'd better take you back to your pasture now."

She tugged on the rope, leading me out of the yard. Once we rounded the corner of the house, she laid a soft hand on my head.

"Don't listen to Martin, Jingle," she whispered with a glance over her shoulder. "He doesn't know what he's talking about. Of course people will always need horses."

# Christmas Eve

The snow began falling again two days before Christmas, the same day Lars took me out to pull home the evergreen tree he'd cut down in the forest. By dawn on Christmas Eve, the fields and pastures were covered in fresh powder nearly as deep as a dog was tall, and I could see every breath puffing out of my nostrils in the crisp, cold air. And more snow was still coming down, fat flakes spinning their way to earth and blending with countless others into a thick white blanket.

Morning chores started extra early, and evening chores took place at a surprising hour not long after noontime. Everyone rushed through the milking, and Anders forgot to give the chickens fresh water until his father reminded him.

"Leave the cows in," Lars told Jonas after a glance outside. "This snow doesn't look likely to stop soon."

Kari heard him and rushed to look out as well. "Isn't it wonderful?" she exclaimed. "It finally feels like Christmas!"

Anders grabbed the strap of harness bells

and shook it. *"Jingle bells, jingle bells, jingle all the way . . . ,"* he sang as the bells rang out.

"Don't smudge the bells!" Kari snatched the strap out of his hands and hung it carefully back in its spot. "They're all ready to put on the harness. Now all that's left is to get Jingle ready."

"Jingle?" Anders widened his eyes as if surprised, though I detected a laugh in his voice. "But I thought we were taking Millie to Mormor and Morfar's today."

"What? No!" Kari whirled to face her father, her eyes suddenly round with worry. "We have to take Jingle, Papa! It's his holiday!"

Her father chuckled and tousled her hair. "Can't you tell by now when your brother is teasing you, child?" he said. "Go ahead and get Jingle ready. I still need to hang out the *julenek* so the wild birds can enjoy their Christmas, too. We'll leave for your grandparents' house in an hour or so. Make sure you allow enough time to change clothes."

"I will, Papa." Kari stuck out her tongue at Anders as he shouted with laughter and scurried out of the barn.

Then she set about giving me the grooming of my life. She started by carefully tapping my hooves one by one, indicating that I should lift each of them up so she could clean them out with a metal pick. After that, she rubbed my legs with a rough cloth until not a speck of dirt or dust remained. Fetching the milking stool, she climbed up and gave me a vigorous rubbing with a currycomb to loosen the dirt in my plush coat. She knocked off that dirt with a stiff-bristled brush, following up with a soft brush to lay the hair back into place.

"You're not that dirty today, Jingle," she commented, sounding a little out of breath after her strenuous efforts. "That's another good thing about snow. It leaves you nice and clean after you roll in it."

Once my coat was spotless, she combed out my mane and tail, dipping the comb in my water bucket to help the coarse strands lie flat. And while she was working, she chattered to me about Christmas plans and all the juicy carrots Mormor would surely have waiting for me when we arrived.

"Maybe she'll even save you some chunks of sugar. Won't that be delicious?" Kari stepped back and looked me over. "Perfect!" she declared.

"Well—almost perfect. I have a surprise for you, Jingle."

She dashed out of the stall and returned a moment later with a small paper bag. She shook the contents out into her hand with a jingle-jangle that made me perk my ears with interest. Millie pulled her nose out of her hay long enough to peer through the slats.

"See?" Kari held up her hand, which was now filled with small silver spheres. "When Asta and I went into town yesterday, I used my egg money to buy these. I'm going to weave them into your mane for extra jingles! Won't everyone be surprised?" She giggled and shook the bells, setting them tinkling again. "I know Mormor will love it!"

Climbing onto the milking stool, she started braiding the tiny bells into my thick mane. Every

time I moved my head, they jingled softly. As Kari's nimble fingers worked the last braid, the door opened with a burst of wind-borne snow. It was Martin, huddled into a long woolen coat.

"Papa just told me what you're doing," he said, stomping the snow off his boots. "You needn't bother, Kari. We're taking the Model T to Morfar and Mormor's."

"What?" Kari shook her head. "Don't be silly. We always take Jingle on Christmas."

"Not this Christmas." Martin's voice sounded very certain. "Morfar and Mormor will want to see the motorcar. Besides, it will be better for the baby. That old carriage is so drafty, and the Model T will get us there much faster. More safely, too."

"No!" Kari exclaimed. "We have to take Jingle. See? He's all ready!"

"Sorry, little sis," Martin said. "You'll see what I mean once you have a ride in the Model T. You know, most of the people in Detroit have already switched from horses to automobiles. Other places, too. It's only a matter of time until everyone follows suit—even in little out-of-the-way spots like this. Now hurry and get dressed so we can go."

Kari dropped her comb in the straw. "I need to talk to Papa and Mama!" she cried. She pushed past Martin and raced out of the barn.

I let out a snort and stepped sideways so quickly that my hoof sent the milking stool clattering against the stall wall. What could have upset Kari so? Seeing her unhappy made me feel unsettled.

Martin shrugged, stepping over to give me a pat on the nose. "Never mind, old boy," he said as he swung my stall door shut. "She'll get over it. And you'll enjoy a rest today, won't you?" He hurried out after his sister.

It was quiet in the barn for a few minutes. Then Kari returned. She was dressed in different clothes, and her hair, which normally seemed to be doing its best to fly off in every direction at once, was now as tidy as my mane. But her eyes were red and her face was sad.

"I'm sorry, Jingle," she cried, rushing into my stall and flinging her arms around my neck, which sent the little bells in my mane ringing. "I tried to convince Papa, but it's no use. They all want to cram themselves into Martin's stupid automobile instead of taking the nice, roomy carriage." She sniffled and stepped back, stroking my nose as I lowered my head to check on her. "It just won't be the same."

Suddenly an intriguing scent reached my nostrils. I flared them, searching for the source. Was it coming from Kari's pocket?

She giggled through her tears as I nudged at

her dress. "Oh, I almost forgot." She reached into the pocket, pulling out a large cookie. "Here, this is for you. Mama's homemade *pepperkake*. Merry Christmas, Jingle."

I tried not to drool as I lipped the cookie off her hand, though it was difficult with the delicious, sugary scent filling my senses. Kari wiped her hand on the straw and pulled out a second cookie. I was still chewing the first, but I leaned forward hopefully.

She giggled again. "Sorry, Jingle," she said. "This one isn't for you."

Stepping out of the stall, she fed half of the second cookie to Millie, then crumbled the rest for the hens, who pecked up the crumbs eagerly.

The taste of the sugary treat lingered pleasantly in my mouth. I leaned my head over the door and watched as Kari checked the chickens' feed pan and water dish. The light in the barn was dim and gray, thanks to the snow still falling steadily outside, but it felt warm and cozy inside, filled with the sounds of the cows chewing their cud, the chickens murmuring softly to themselves, and Kari humming under her breath.

The door banged open, startling everyone. It was Anders, red-cheeked and breathless.

"Bring a horse!" he called to Kari. "The Model T's stuck!"

# In the Barn

A barking dog burst into the barn right behind Anders, followed by Lars. "What's going on?" Kari exclaimed, hurrying to meet her father. "What does Anders mean, the Model T's stuck?"

Lars removed his hat and shook off the snow.

"Martin was going to pull the car closer to the house so we wouldn't have to walk through the weather," he said. "But the snow covered up the ditch by the road, and Martin forgot it was there. He backed the automobile right into it, and he can't get it out."

Anders was already grabbing my plow harness off its hook. "Never mind," he said. "Jingle can pull it out. Can't you, boy?"

I didn't understand what was going on, but I understood what it meant when Lars tossed the harness over my back and started buckling the straps. I was going to work.

*What's happening?* Millie peered at me through the slats. *Why are they putting on the plow harness? You can't plow in the snow!*

*It's better not to wonder about the ways of*

*humans,* I reminded her. *I'll find out soon enough what they have in mind.*

Kari helped her father and brother finish attaching the hames and doing up the last of the straps. Then Lars led me toward the door.

"Grab the chains," he told Anders.

"I'll help carry them," Kari volunteered.

We stepped outside. The snow was falling steadily, and I had to blink more frequently than usual to remove the flakes that seemed determined to gather on my eyelashes. I walked across the stable yard beside Lars, my hooves leaving deep tracks in the powder and the bells in my mane tinkling with each step.

When we rounded the corner of the house, several humans were gathered in the front yard. The horseless carriage was there, too. It was tipped up in a strange way, its front wheels hanging uselessly above the snow. I lifted my head in surprise as I saw it looking so much different than the last time I'd seen it.

"Come along, Jingle." Jonas hurried toward me, followed by Martin and Hanne.

"Do you think he can get it out?" Frida called from the front porch.

She was taking shelter there with Asta beside her. Pearl and the baby were nowhere in sight.

Kari had just struggled into the yard, dragging a length of heavy chain. "Don't worry. Jingle can do it!" she called back to her mother.

Lars led me closer. "Take a look, fella," he said, stroking my neck as we neared the horseless carriage. "It's just another type of carriage for you to pull, all right?"

"Don't worry, Papa." Kari dropped her chain in the snow nearby. "Jingle isn't afraid of anything."

Lars smiled. "All right, then. Let's hitch him up."

"We'll attach the chains first," Jonas said, grabbing the chain Kari had dropped. "Bring that one over here, Anders."

"Be careful of the headlights." Martin hurried forward. "Here, let me do it. . . ."

The men fussed over the chains and the horse-less carriage for a little while. I stood patiently, waiting for them to tell me what to do. Frida tried to call Kari and Anders over to wait on the porch, but both of them refused, flitting around in the snow like moths.

Finally Jonas and Martin attached the chains to my harness. Lars took hold of my noseband.

"Ready, Jingle?" he said. "This might be a tough job, but I know you can do it. Giddyup, now!"

Recognizing the command as well as the tug on the noseband, I took a step forward, and then another. I felt the weight of the load settle against my collar as the chains straightened and tightened.

"Go on, Jingle." Kari danced beside me, clapping her hands, though it made only a muffled sound through her mittens. "You can do it!"

I leaned forward, gathering my muscles. The load behind me was much heavier than plowing in even the worst soil, and it didn't seem ready to roll as easily as the carriage or the wagon. Still, I knew I could make it move.

"Go, Jingle!" Anders added his voice to his sister's.

My hooves dug through the snow and into the frozen ground beneath, seeking purchase. My shoulder muscles strained against the collar, and my hindquarters bunched in effort. Finally I felt the load shift.

"There!" Anders cried. "He's got it—it's moving!"

"Careful." Martin had stepped away, looking from me to my load and back again. "Don't let him pull too fast."

"Stand back, son," Lars said. Then he clucked to me. "Walk on, Jingle. Good man."

I took another step. The load behind me moved again. Another step. This time it seemed easier.

"Here it comes!" Kari cried.

I looked back without turning my head. The dark mass of my load was sliding forward. The wheels touched down and disappeared into the snow. A moment later, most of the pressure was gone.

"It's rolling!" Jonas cried. "Quick, get the brake before it rolls right into him!"

There was a flurry of movement as Martin

leaped toward the automobile. Lars asked me to halt, and I stood patiently, blowing out heavy breaths into the cold air. My flanks were damp with sweat beneath my thick coat, but I was satisfied. I'd done my job, and my master seemed pleased.

Lars unhitched me and walked me back to the barn with Kari at his side. The dogs all followed us as well.

"Good boy, Jingle," Kari said as we walked. "See, Papa? He's much better than that silly motorcar, isn't he?"

"Hush, child." Her father swung open the barn door and led me inside. "Your Jingle has done a good job. Now it's his turn to rest and enjoy Christmas."

The dogs raced into the barn ahead of us.

Dash chased the cat from her spot on a low straw bale; she leaped easily higher up the stack and hissed at the terrier. The other dogs began snuffling at the ground for any bits of grain the hens might have left there.

Kari and her father quickly removed my harness. "Never mind wiping it down at the moment," Lars said. "We'll just hang it up and take care of it after the holiday."

"Yes, Papa." Kari carried the bridle and plow lines, while her father took the rest.

Soon I was back in my stall. Kari and her father worked together to give me a quick grooming to clean away the sweat before it could give me a chill. After that, Kari tossed a fresh pile of hay to Millie and to me while Lars checked on the cows.

The door opened, and Anders peeked in. "Are you coming? Pearl and the baby are already waiting in the motorcar, and Mama doesn't want them to get cold."

"Coming." Lars glanced around. "I think the animals are all settled in. Let's go, Kari."

Kari dashed over to my stall. "Merry Christmas, Jingle," she said. "I'll make sure to bring home some carrots from Mormor for your Christmas treat."

Then they were gone.

*Where did you go?* Millie looked through the slats with curious eyes and bits of hay dribbling from her mouth. *What happened? Did you plow the snow?*

*No,* I said. *It was a different kind of work today. I pulled the horseless carriage.*

*What?* She sounded surprised and a little confused. *How do you mean?*

I told her what had happened as best I understood it. *The thing was difficult to move at first, I* finished. *But then it became easier.*

*Like pulling the plow from untouched, rocky ground into a well-worked field?* she wondered.

*Much like that, yes.* I reached down for a mouthful of hay. *Perhaps that's why horseless carriages usually move by themselves. They seem tricky to pull. The milk wagon is a much simpler kind of creature.*

*Indeed.* Millie snorted. *But difficult enough to get moving when it's loaded full!*

*Never mind. The humans are gone, and we don't have to worry about work right now,* I said. *This hay is good, isn't it?*

After that, the barn settled into a peaceful hush. The dogs had finished scavenging for food and were curled up in the straw. Millie and I were chewing our hay contentedly, and on the other side of the barn the cows were doing the same, their warmth heating the barn until it felt more like spring than winter inside. The hens were doing as they always did, pecking or roosting or fluffing their feathers with their beaks as evening drew closer. The cat was purring atop her throne of straw and hay. Outside the windows, the snow continued to fall, and a gust of wind occasionally rattled the glass, but inside we were warm and sleepy and content.

Was this what Christmas was like for humans, too? I wasn't sure, but I hoped so, for it was as

pleasant as I could imagine. Work was satisfying, but it was good to rest, too.

At some point I dozed off with my nose in the corner of the stall. I was startled awake by the bang of the door swinging open.

*What is it? There's a noise!* Millie cried, while the dogs started barking: *Humans! Humans!*

I stepped to the door of my stall and saw that Kari and her father had just rushed in. Both of them were out of breath and covered in a layer of snow. Kari's cheeks were bright red with cold.

"Jingle, we need you again!" she cried, hurrying toward me with the dogs leaping around her feet. "There was ice on the road, and the Model T slid into a snowbank. It's stuck!"

# Dashing Through the Snow

"Stop talking to Jingle, and help me with the harness, child." Lars sounded anxious as he rushed toward the back of the barn. "It's getting colder every moment, and we don't want the baby to get chilled."

Kari nodded as he disappeared into the

harness room. But she loved to talk nearly as much as the dogs did, and couldn't resist whispering to me as she led me out of the stall and tied me in the open area, where it was easier to put on the harness.

"Oh, it was terrible, Jingle!" she said. "I don't know how Martin could see a thing through the falling snow, and it's getting deeper all the time on the roads. The motorcar's wheels were sliding all over even before we crashed." She glanced at her father, who was returning with the harness slung over his shoulders. "Papa doesn't think the Model T would be able to make it through the drifts much longer even if we could get it pushed back up on the road. That's why we came for you." She patted my rump as she hurried past to help her father.

Lars stopped short when he saw me. "Oh—
I was thinking we would take Millie this time,"
he told Kari. "Jingle has already done his share
of work for today by pulling the automobile out of
the ditch. Besides, the mare will get us back to
the others faster."

"But we have to take Jingle!" Kari protested.
"It's Christmas! I'm sure he won't mind the extra
work. And he might not be fast, but he's steady. It
will be safer for the baby to have him pulling us
on the snowy roads."

Lars glanced at me. I stared back at him,
waiting to be told what to do. Finally he sighed
and smiled.

"I suppose you're right," he told his daughter
as he gave me a pat. "Jingle is indeed the steadier
horse, and the stronger one as well. We might

need those qualities today." He glanced at the window. "Let's hurry, then."

Kari nodded, looking relieved and happy. "Ready, Jingle? We've got to be quick. The baby will be cold, and Mormor and Morfar will be wondering where we are."

When the harness was on, Lars led me over to the large bob-runner sleigh parked at one end of the aisle. There hadn't been enough snow yet that year to use it, but Lars had kept it clean and ready to go as he did with all his equipment. He and Kari hitched me to it, then helped push it over the rough barn floor toward the door. The dogs weren't much help, though they thought they were. Dash repeatedly jumped in and out of the sleigh, while the others barked, *Something's happening! Something's happening!*

The snow was coming down harder now, and a steady wind blew it diagonally into my face. I laid my ears back and slitted my eyes against it as we stepped out of the barn. Angry gray storm clouds hid the pale winter sky, making it seem dark even though the sun wouldn't set for another hour or more. The sleigh's runners slid more easily once they touched the snow, and I barely had to lean against the collar at all to keep it moving. Lars led me to a flat spot and asked me to halt.

"Help me fetch the blankets," he said to Kari. "We'll need them today." He patted my neck. "Stay here, Jingle."

I stood still as the humans disappeared back into the barn. They reemerged a moment later, fuzzy blankets piled in their arms. They tossed

the blankets into the sleigh, then climbed in
themselves. Kari settled herself beside her father
on the front bench as he picked up the reins.

"Giddyup, Jingle!" she called. "Let's go!"

I stepped forward. The sleigh slid easily behind me. It took little effort to pull it across the yard toward the road. As I settled into a rhythm, my head nodded in time with my walk. The tiny bells Kari had woven into my mane started to jingle softly.

Suddenly Kari let out a cry of dismay. "Wait!" she said. "Whoa, Jingle! We forgot the bells!"

"Never mind," Lars told her as I came to a halt. "We don't have time to fuss with bells right now."

"But it's Christmas!" Before her father could say another word, Kari jumped down from the sleigh. She raced back to the barn and soon returned with the harness bells.

Lars sighed and climbed down. "Here, let me help you. . . ."

The two of them quickly attached the bells

to the harness. "There!" Kari said, stepping back and wiping the snow off her face. "*Now* we're ready to go!"

Once again, she and her father climbed into the sleigh. Once again, Lars picked up the reins. Once again, I heard Kari's musical voice call out, "Giddyup, Jingle!"

We set off, picking up a slow trot as soon as we were on the road. The bells jingled on the harness, mixing with the softer sound of the ones in my mane. My breath puffed out evenly, blending with the fallen snow, and my muscles warmed up and hummed with the work. Some of the snow had been cleared from the road surface, but enough fresh powder had fallen for the runners to slide easily along. Once or twice we hit a bare spot, but all it took was a little extra effort, and we scraped over and back onto the snow.

Kari and her father didn't talk much. When I looked back, I saw that they were huddled together beneath one of the blankets. But a few times, I heard Kari humming. I wasn't sure, but I thought I recognized the tune she'd been singing so often lately, the one with my name in it.

We followed the winding country lane out to the main road. I remembered that this was the spot where a horseless carriage had once passed so close that it had nearly touched my muzzle. But there were no horseless carriages on the road today. In fact, there wasn't much traffic at all. A light, fancy cutter passed in the opposite direction, being pulled by an elegant blood bay mare trotting at a good clip. A couple of larger sleighs also passed us as we started down the road, the occupants waving from beneath layers of blankets and winter clothes. I nodded to one of the horses, a stout draft cross gelding I knew from the hitching rail outside of the church. His breath puffed into the air as he snorted a greeting in return, and then he was gone, trotting steadily in the other direction.

I turned all my attention back to my job. The sleigh was less stable to pull than the carriage or wagon, prone to sliding back and forth at the slightest change in the road surface. So I was careful to stay as straight as possible and maintain a steady pace. My trot wasn't fast, but it covered the ground well enough. Snowballs formed occasionally in my hooves, causing brief annoyances before they eventually popped loose.

"Are we there yet?" Kari asked after a while.

"I think it was somewhere just after the old gray barn that we hit the ice."

"Yes, we should see them soon." Lars tugged on the reins to slow me down.

I settled back into a walk, glad for the breather. When we rounded the next bend, I saw the horseless carriage—well, part of it, in any case. The front end was buried in a large drift, with the back half sticking out into the road. The family was standing nearby, huddled together for warmth. Pearl was holding the baby, with Martin's coat draped over her. Martin himself was stamping and slapping his arms against his body, trying to stay warm.

Everyone cheered when they saw me coming. "Jingle Bells to the rescue!" Anders cried, racing over to give me a pat.

"Oh, thank goodness!" Frida hurried after her youngest son. "Come, Pearl. Get yourself settled in the middle, and we'll get a blanket for you and baby Eva. . . ."

"Don't forget to get the gifts out of the motorcar," Hanne said.

"And the food." Jonas licked his lips. "Mama's Christmas cookies and rice pudding must be frozen by now!"

"Never mind." Asta hurried over and grabbed a package off the seat of the horseless carriage. "They'll thaw well enough once we're in a nice, warm house."

A few moments of hustle and bustle followed. I stood patiently, glad of the chance to rest, even though the air had grown colder as dusk crept closer and parts of me were damp from exertion.

Meanwhile the humans scrambled in and out of the sleigh, settling themselves on the narrow benches. As soon as his wife and baby were tucked in with one of the warm lap blankets, Martin came forward to see me.

"Thanks, Jingle," he said softly, rubbing my nose. He shot a sheepish look at the horseless

carriage. "Maybe it's a good thing there are still a few fine horses like you around after all."

It was a tight squeeze, but everyone was able to fit in the sleigh, though Anders and Jonas rode hanging off the sides, balancing on the tops of the runners. Lars pulled Kari up beside him, then picked up the reins.

"Giddyup, Jingle!" he said. "Let's get out of here!"

I stepped forward, my bells jingling in time with my gait, and we set off for Mormor and Morfar's house.

## Jingle All the Way

As soon as I pulled into the snow-covered yard, Mormor and Morfar burst out of the house. "Oh, thank goodness!" Mormor cried, lifting her skirts as she stepped off the porch into the snow. "I was about to send Thomas out with the sleigh to search for you."

"No need, Mormor, we're here!" Anders cried as he and Jonas jumped down from the sleigh as nimbly as squirrels. Anders rushed over to hug Mormor, while Jonas stretched out a hand to help his mother out of the sleigh.

For my part, I was glad to stand still a moment and rest. It had been a long journey through the blowing snow.

Frida ran a hand along my neck as she stepped past me to embrace Morfar, who had followed his wife down into the yard. "Oh, Papa!" Frida exclaimed. "You'll never believe what happened. . . ."

All the humans started chattering, describing their adventures. At the end, Jonas gave me a stout pat on the shoulder.

"Not to worry," he said. "Jingle saved the day!"

"Wonderful." Mormor stroked my nose. "I've always said he was a special one. But come—let's get that baby inside and warm ourselves with some lovely spiced cider. . . ."

"Poor Jingle shouldn't have to stand out in the snow," Morfar added. "I'll help you unhitch him. He can warm up in the barn with Queenie."

"I'll help, too," Kari offered.

Her mother frowned. "No, you should come inside and let your father and grandfather handle it—you must be exhausted after running all that way through the snow to fetch the sleigh."

"It's all right, Mama," Kari insisted. "Jingle worked harder than I did. I want to make sure he's settled in the barn."

Frida opened her mouth as if to protest further, but her husband laid a gentle hand on her

arm. "Just leave it, my dearest," he said. "The girl
will be all right. She wants to help."

"Fine," Frida said with a sigh. "But hurry and
get inside, all of you! It will be dark soon, and
only growing colder."

She headed into the house with the others.

Kari, Lars, Morfar, and Jonas stayed behind. Lars
and Jonas unhooked me from the sleigh; then Kari
took hold of the bridle and led me out from between
the shafts. We followed Morfar through the gate
into the paddock where Queenie lived, though the
mare was nowhere in sight at the moment.

"We put Queenie inside when the snow started blowing earlier," Morfar said as we all crossed the snow-covered paddock. "It's not a night for man nor beast out here, Christmas Eve or not."

He led the way to the small barn at the back of the paddock. It was not much like our barn at home, being little more than a large shed with two stalls and a tiny loft overhead. But when we stepped inside, it felt warm and cozy. Queenie glanced up from a tasty-looking pile of hay and snorted in surprise.

*Jingle!* she said. *I was not expecting any visitors to be out in this storm.*

*It's Christmas Eve,* I told her. *That seems to be an important matter for humans. My master and his family were quite determined to come here by whatever means were needed. In this case, it meant me pulling them here in the sleigh.*

*I see.* The pretty liver chestnut mare looked impressed. *Oh, dear, what's that in your mane? There can't be brambles along the roads at this time of year!*

I shook my head to set my bells jingling. I'd grown so used to having them there that I hardly heard them anymore.

*No, they're bells—like the ones the humans sometimes hang on the harness,* I explained. *I don't know why they do it. But the sound is quite pleasant, isn't it?*

*I suppose,* Queenie replied, though she seemed dubious.

"Okay, Jingle," Lars said. "Let's get you

settled in for a nice rest. Can you get the girth, Kari?"

"Yes, Papa." Kari's nimble fingers quickly unhooked the buckles at my belly.

I stood quietly while the humans worked together to remove the harness. Then Kari led me into the empty stall beside Queenie. Several hens were roosting there, their feathers puffed out against the cold and their eyes sleepy. They mumbled and chuckled in annoyance as Morfar shooed them out into the open area in front of the stalls.

"Poor birdies," Kari said with a laugh. "Jingle is stealing your bed, and on Christmas!"

"Never mind. They'll find another place to sleep." Lars reached into a metal can and scattered some corn on the ground.

That woke the hens well enough. They dashed over and started pecking at the kernels.

Meanwhile Jonas was scrambling up the ladder to the loft. He tossed down a pile of hay, which Lars speared with a pitchfork and set before me.

*You'll like the hay,* Queenie told me, taking another mouthful from her own pile. *It has a fair amount of alfalfa in it.*

*Good. Though I'm hungry enough to eat plain straw,* I said, diving into the hay. Indeed, the hay and grain I'd enjoyed back in my home barn seemed very long ago.

Kari gave me a pat. "There you go, Jingle," she said. "Enjoy your Christmas dinner."

"Come, child." Morfar was heading for the door, followed by Lars and Jonas. "Leave the

· 151 ·

horses to their rest, and let's go in and start Christmas."

Soon the humans were gone. Queenie and I stood in our side-by-side stalls, munching steadily at our hay. The chilly air that had blown in with me was soon overtaken by the heat of our bodies. The hens ate every bit of corn they could find, and then, after quite a bit of squabbling, finally settled themselves on a stack of hay bales. They spent a few more moments shifting their weight and pecking at one another and grooming their feathers, but eventually they dropped off to sleep.

After that, the tiny barn was peaceful. A large ginger tomcat crept in after a while through a hole in a board, pausing to stare at me in the curious way cats have. He shook the snow off his fur and leaped gracefully onto the riding saddle resting on a stand near the feed bins. He spent a few moments grooming himself, then curled up and joined the chickens in sleep.

I continued eating. My hunger had subsided, so I spent more time picking through the hay, moving the rough stems aside in search of the tastier bits of alfalfa. I'd just found another mouthful when I heard a pleasant sound outside, louder than the constant breathing of the wind.

Queenie lifted her head from her hay and pricked her small ears. *What is that?* she wondered.

*It sounds like humans,* I noted, stepping forward to look out of the stall.

The barn door opened, admitting a blast of

cold air along with the entire group of humans. Kari was right at the front, wrapped in her coat and with a big smile on her face. Beside her were Anders and Hanne. Martin was holding the baby just behind them, while Pearl, Asta, Jonas, Frida, Lars, Mormor, and Morfar gathered around as well.

All of them were speaking at once—but no, it wasn't speaking exactly. It was the other kind of sound, the one Kari sometimes made while we were riding out through the forest or fields. The humans called it singing, and it was pleasing to my ears. Queenie seemed to agree, for she left her hay and stepped to the front of her stall as well. Even the cat woke up and listened, though the hens merely muttered uncertainly and tucked their heads farther into their feathers.

The singing stopped all at once. Kari glanced over her shoulder at the others, still smiling.

"All right," she said. "Let's do a special song for Jingle now."

She lifted a hand, and all together, the entire group burst into song once again:

*"Jingle bells, jingle bells,*
*Jingle all the way.*
*Oh, what joy it is to ride*
*In a one-horse open sleigh. . . ."*

As they finished, Mormor stepped forward. My ears pricked toward her, and my mouth started watering as I recognized what she was holding. Carrots! A lot of them!

"Merry Christmas, Jingle," she said, with

a kind smile that made her eyes crinkle at the edges. "You didn't think I'd forgotten your favorite treat, did you?"

I eagerly accepted the carrot she held out for me, my teeth crunching down on its juicy sweetness. Anders took a few carrots from Mormor's hand to give to Queenie, who was hanging her head out over her door and nickering.

"Jingle definitely deserves a Christmas treat, don't you think, Martin?" Kari slid her gaze toward her eldest brother, who was bouncing the baby in his arms. "We might never have made it here if we'd had to rely on the motorcar."

Martin sighed and smiled as the rest of the family laughed.

"Indeed, young man." Morfar clapped Martin

on the shoulder. "Are you ready to give up helping Mr. Ford build those silly automobiles and come back to do some real work on the farm?"

"Let's not go too far, Morfar," Martin said with a chuckle. "The Model T might not be perfect, but I still believe it will change the world."

"If you say so." Morfar winked at Kari. "But I hope you'll admit now that a good horse still has its uses."

Martin shifted the baby to one arm, stepping forward to give me a pat. "Of course," he said. "I'm glad Jingle was there to rescue us today, and I'm not ashamed to admit it."

I nosed at his coat, wondering if there were any more carrots hidden in the pockets. My whiskers brushed against baby Eva's pudgy arm, and she gurgled and batted at me.

"Look!" Anders exclaimed with a laugh. "Little Eva likes horses, too!"

Martin grinned. "Of course she does. Here you go, Eva—want to have a ride on the nice horsie?"

He ducked under the wooden plank that served as a stall barrier and swung the baby up onto my broad back, keeping one hand on her chest and one behind her neck to steady her. My ears swiveled back, but otherwise I remained perfectly still. I could feel the baby's warm, slightly damp weight resting on me and her tiny hands patting at my withers. She cooed and kicked her small legs.

"Look!" Kari exclaimed. "She wants Jingle to giddyup!"

I recognized the command, of course.

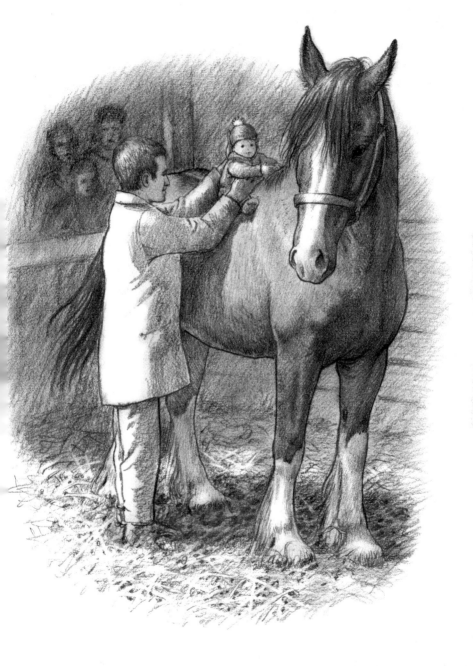

Normally when I heard it, I stepped off immediately. But I could tell that in this case, Kari hadn't meant it that way, and so I remained as still as ever.

Pearl was watching from outside the stall, her expression nervous. "All right, that's enough, Martin," she said. "We don't want the baby to get chilled. Shall we all go back inside?"

Martin pulled Eva off my back and handed her across the barrier to his wife before ducking out of the stall himself. "That's fine. I'd like another helping of Mormor's roasted pork and sauerkraut anyway." He patted his stomach and headed over to swing open the door.

Most of the humans hurried out with him. Only Kari lingered, slipping into my stall and running her hands up my neck until I lowered my head toward her.

"Here you go, Jingle," she whispered. "I snitched this for you—don't let Mormor see."

She held out something on her palm. It was too small to see properly, but my nose told me it was sweet and good. I lipped it off her hand and crunched it, and my mouth was filled with a taste even sweeter than carrots.

"It's some sugar candy her neighbors brought over—I hope you like it," Kari told me, rubbing my nose as I chewed. Then she wrapped her arms around my head, resting her face against my cheek. "Merry Christmas, Jingle Bells."

# APPENDIX

## MORE ABOUT THE
## CLYDESDALE HORSE

## American Immigrant

The Clydesdale horse takes its name from the region of Scotland where the breed was first developed. Throughout the nineteenth century,

Clydesdale horses became popular not only in their own area, but throughout Scotland, the rest of the United Kingdom, and the world. Clydesdales were introduced to the United States around the time of the Civil War, and the first American breeders' association dedicated to the Clydesdale horse was founded in 1879. This association is known today as the Clydesdale Breeders of the U.S.A.

## The Clydesdale Breed Grows Up... and Up... and Up

In the early days, Clydesdales were stocky and strong but tended to be shorter than other draft breeds such as the Percheron, Shire, and Belgian draft. It wasn't until the mid-twentieth century that breeders began selecting taller horses. These

days, Clydesdales can stand up to eighteen hands or even more. The record for the world's tallest living horse was held for a while by a Clydesdale named Remington, who stood at twenty hands. Now that's a big horse!

## A Versatile Worker

Today the Clydesdale remains a popular breed. Bay horses with white on the face and legs tend to be preferred by many enthusiasts, but Clydesdales can also come in roan, chestnut, black, and gray. They are still used for their time-honored jobs of farmwork, carriage driving, and heavy hauling, and are a popular sight in advertising and other media. But these days they are also sought after as parade horses, riding horses, and show horses. They are often crossbred with light horses to create a midsized riding horse.

## MORE ABOUT KARI AND JINGLE'S WORLD

## Scandinavian Traditions

As Norwegian immigrants, Kari's family retains some of the customs and traditions of the old country. This includes their celebrations during the Christmas season, known as *Jul* (pronounced like the English version of the word, *Yule*).

One of these traditions is *Lussinatten,* which falls on December 13, once considered the longest night of the year. Trolls and other evil spirits were free to roam the earth and punish humans who did any work on that day. It was also believed that farm animals could talk to each other on *Lussinatten* night, and because of this, their owners gave the animals extra feed.

In the twentieth century, *Lussinatten* was combined with St. Lucia's Day, a church holiday that is still celebrated on December 13. Throughout Norway and the other Scandinavian countries, girls are chosen to portray St. Lucia. They wear white gowns, red sashes, and crowns of candles. The girls lead processions, hand out special "Lucia buns," and sing songs to honor the saint.

Another holiday tradition is the *julenek*, a sheaf of wheat, oats, or other grains. Norwegians hang the *julenek* outside so that the wild birds can have their own Christmas feast.

# HORSE POWER VERSUS HORSEPOWER

In 1915, there were still well over twenty million horses at work in the United States. However, the automobile was rapidly increasing in popularity and accessibility.

The Model T, the car Martin brings home, was considered the first truly affordable automobile, thanks largely to Henry Ford's groundbreaking assembly-line method of building them. In 1915, a standard Model T cost $440.

Of course, $440 was a lot more money back then. Even so, it was said that an assembly-line worker at one of Ford's plants could buy a Model T with just a few months' pay. (Not much more than the price of a good horse!)

The Model T was produced between 1908 and 1927. Eventually, motorized vehicles replaced horses for almost all uses in the developed world, though Clydesdales and other breeds are still used for recreational driving today.

## GALLOP AHEAD FOR GREAT ACTIVITIES!

· Make some of the Norwegian cookies
and crafts Kari's family prepares for *Jul*.

· Test your horse sense with
Horse Diaries trivia questions.

· And learn to draw Jingle Bells from
illustrator Ruth Sanderson herself!

**Activities**

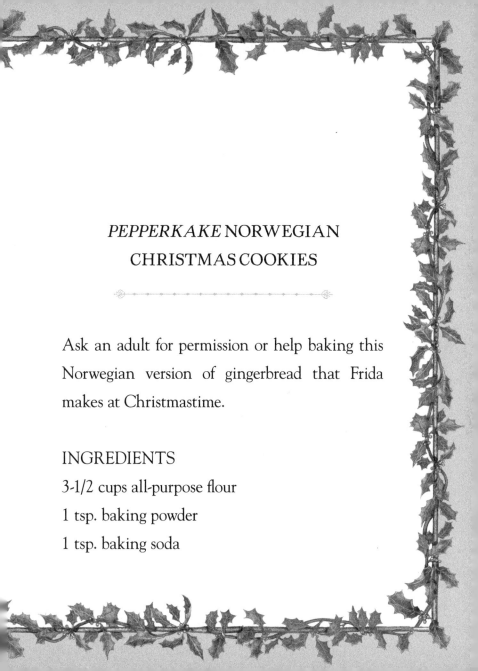

## *PEPPERKAKE* NORWEGIAN CHRISTMAS COOKIES

Ask an adult for permission or help baking this Norwegian version of gingerbread that Frida makes at Christmastime.

### INGREDIENTS
3-1/2 cups all-purpose flour
1 tsp. baking powder
1 tsp. baking soda

1 tsp. black pepper

1 tsp. ground cardamom

1 tsp. cinnamon

1/2 tsp. ground ginger

1 cup (2 sticks) butter, softened

1 cup sugar

1/2 cup cream

In a large bowl, mix flour, baking powder, baking soda, and all the spices.

In another bowl, beat butter and sugar together until creamy and fluffy. Add cream and beat again.

Gradually add the dry ingredients to the wet ones, about 1/2 cup at a time, mixing well after each addition.

Form the dough into a ball. Wrap in plastic wrap and chill in the refrigerator overnight.

Preheat oven to 350 degrees. Roll out dough until it is about 1/4 inch thick. Cut out shapes with cookie cutters. If you want to use your cookies as Christmas tree ornaments, cut a hole out of the top of each cookie.

Place on lightly greased cookie sheets and bake for 10 to 12 minutes, or until golden brown on the bottom. Enjoy!

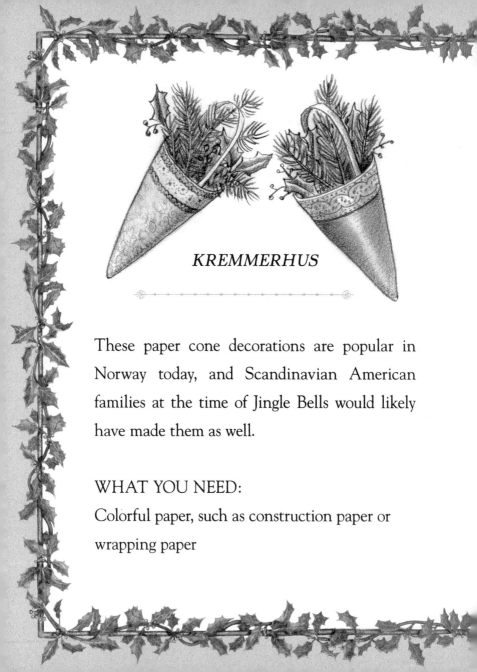

## KREMMERHUS

These paper cone decorations are popular in Norway today, and Scandinavian American families at the time of Jingle Bells would likely have made them as well.

WHAT YOU NEED:
Colorful paper, such as construction paper or wrapping paper

Scissors

Glue stick or stapler

Hole punch

Ribbon, yarn, string, or wire

Fun things to put in your *kremmerhus*!

Cut your paper into a large rectangle, if it is not already a rectangular shape. If you are using wrapping paper or other thin paper, you may want to glue it to a stronger piece of construction paper or poster board of equal size. Roll the paper into a cone. Glue or staple the ends together to keep the shape.

With the hole punch, make a hole in each side at the top of the cone. Cut your ribbon, yarn, string, or wire to the length you want your *kremmerhus* to hang. Tie each end through the holes in the cone, and you have a handle!

Fill your *kremmerhus* any way you want. You could use pinecones, greens, holly, garland, cotton balls, candy, or little toys. Hang it on the Christmas tree, in an entryway, or anywhere else you might want a festive decoration!

## HORSE DIARIES TRIVIA

Have you read all the books in the Horse Diaries series? Test your knowledge with these questions about the stories and breeds of horses in your favorite books.

1. In *Elska*, who shows Elska how to tölt—to do one of the special gaits Icelandic horses are known for?

(a) Amma    (b) Tappi

(c) Tassi    (d) Leira

2. What is the Icelandic word for the yearly roundup of horses, sheep, and other livestock?

   (a) *Gullfoss*   (b) *Geysir*

   (c) *sunnudagur*   (d) *rettir*

3. In *Bell's Star*, where does Star bring Eliza?

   (a) Mexico   (b) Maine

   (c) Canada   (d) New Hampshire

4. The Morgan is considered America's _____ horse breed.

   (a) oldest   (b) biggest

   (c) most beautiful   (d) shyest

5. In *Koda*, what animal is Koda trying to outrun when he gets lost?

   (a) bear   (b) snake

   (c) porcupine   (d) cougar

6. When the quarter horse breed was first developed, what was it best known for?

    (a) speed    (b) jumping

    (c) dressage    (d) an extra gait

7. In *Maestoso Petra*, what sweet treat does Petra always smell coming from the bakery in Vienna?

    (a) carrot cake    (b) Linzer torte

    (c) apple strudel    (d) doughnuts

8. In which of the airs above the ground that Lipizzaners perform does a horse jump in place, then kick out his hind legs in midair?

    (a) the *courbette*    (b) the *capriole*

    (c) the *levade*    (d) the *croupade*

9. In *Golden Sun*, what medicinal plant does Golden Sun find to save Pale Moon?

    (a) kinnikinnick   (b) kouse root

    (c) coltsfoot   (d) willow bark

10. Which native people bred the Appaloosa horse?

    (a) Cherokee   (b) Navajo

    (c) Lakota   (d) Nez Perce

11. In *Yatimah*, what kind of danger does Yatimah help Safiya survive?

    (a) sandstorm   (b) raid

    (c) earthquake   (d) heatstroke

12. What did the Bedouin people often feed their Arabian horses when grass was scarce?

    (a) figs   (b) oats

    (c) dates   (d) bran

13. In *Risky Chance*, what nickname do the grooms give Chance before he's trained?

       (a) Hurricane    (b) Lucifer

       (c) Young Fury    (d) Gray Devil

14. About 95 percent of Thoroughbreds can trace their roots back to what horse?

       (a) Valentine Lassie    (b) Man o' War

       (c) Eclipse    (d) Bulle Rock

15. In *Black Cloud*, which foal starts out as the bully of the herd?

       (a) Abril    (b) Sota

       (c) Omar    (d) Will

16. Velma Bronn Johnston, who brought the plight of the mustangs to national attention, is better known by what name?

(a) Wild Horse Annie    (b) Suzy Rider

(c) Crazy Horse    (d) Mustang Sally

17. In *Tennessee Rose*, what is the name of the wise old horse who teaches Rosie much of what she knows?

(a) Dasher    (b) Charger

(c) Knightley    (d) Rigby

18. Which horse first became known for the running walk, which gives the Tennessee Walking Horse its name?

(a) Black Allan    (b) Traveller

(c) Bald Stockings    (d) Trigger

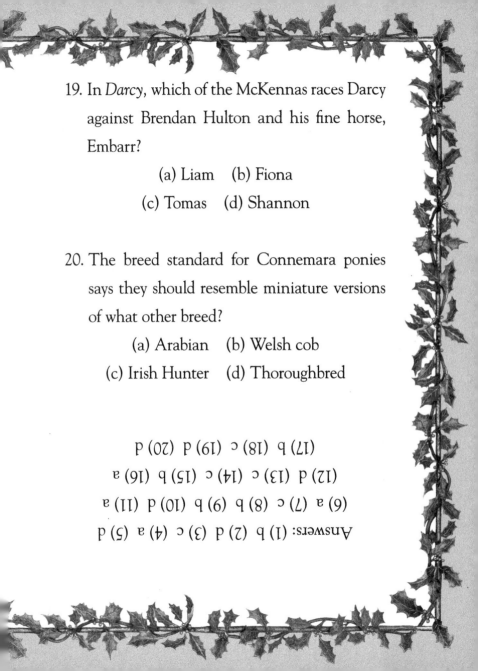

19. In *Darcy*, which of the McKennas races Darcy against Brendan Hulton and his fine horse, Embarr?

> (a) Liam   (b) Fiona
> (c) Tomas   (d) Shannon

20. The breed standard for Connemara ponies says they should resemble miniature versions of what other breed?

> (a) Arabian   (b) Welsh cob
> (c) Irish Hunter   (d) Thoroughbred

Answers: (1) b (2) d (3) c (4) a (5) d
(6) a (7) c (8) b (9) b (10) d (11) a
(12) d (13) c (14) c (15) b (16) a
(17) b (18) c (19) d (20) d

# HOW TO DRAW JINGLE BELLS

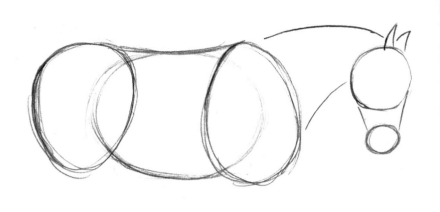

Sanderson

# ABOUT THE AUTHOR

Catherine Hapka has written more than 150 books for children and young adults, including many about horses. A lifelong horse lover, she rides several times a week and appreciates horses of all breeds. In addition to writing and riding, she enjoys all kinds of animals, reading, gardening, music, and travel. She lives on a small farm in Chester County, Pennsylvania, which she shares with a horse, three goats, a small flock of chickens, and too many cats.

# ABOUT THE ILLUSTRATOR

Ruth Sanderson grew up with a love for horses. She has illustrated and retold many fairy tales and likes to feature horses in them whenever possible. Her book about a magical horse, *The Golden Mare, the Firebird, and the Magic Ring*, won the Texas Bluebonnet Award.

Ruth and her daughter have two horses, an Appaloosa named Thor and a quarter horse named Gabriel. She lives with her family in Massachusetts.

To find out more about her adventures with horses and the research she does to create Horse Diaries illustrations, visit her website, ruthsanderson.com.

# Collect all the books in the Horse Diaries series!

 Elska

 Bell's Star

 Koda

 Maestoso Petra

 Golden Sun

 Yatimah

 Risky Chance

 Black Cloud

 Tennessee Rose

 Darcy

 Jingle Bells